ROOSEVELT
AND THE MAGIC BOX
Adventure on Thunder Island

R. ROGERS, F. SPARACINO, & S. VANVOORHIS
ILLUSTRATED BY MICHAEL MIRACLE

BOOK BUDDY™

This book is dedicated to Mario and Betty Turco
for all their love, support, and caring.
With special thanks to Tim Ford
for his help and creative imagination.

Library of Congress Catalog Card Number: 95–83842

ISBN 0–9642564–8–7

Printed in the United States of America

1 3 5 7 9 10 8 6 4 2
PC

ROOSEVELT
AND THE MAGIC BOX
Adventure on Thunder Island

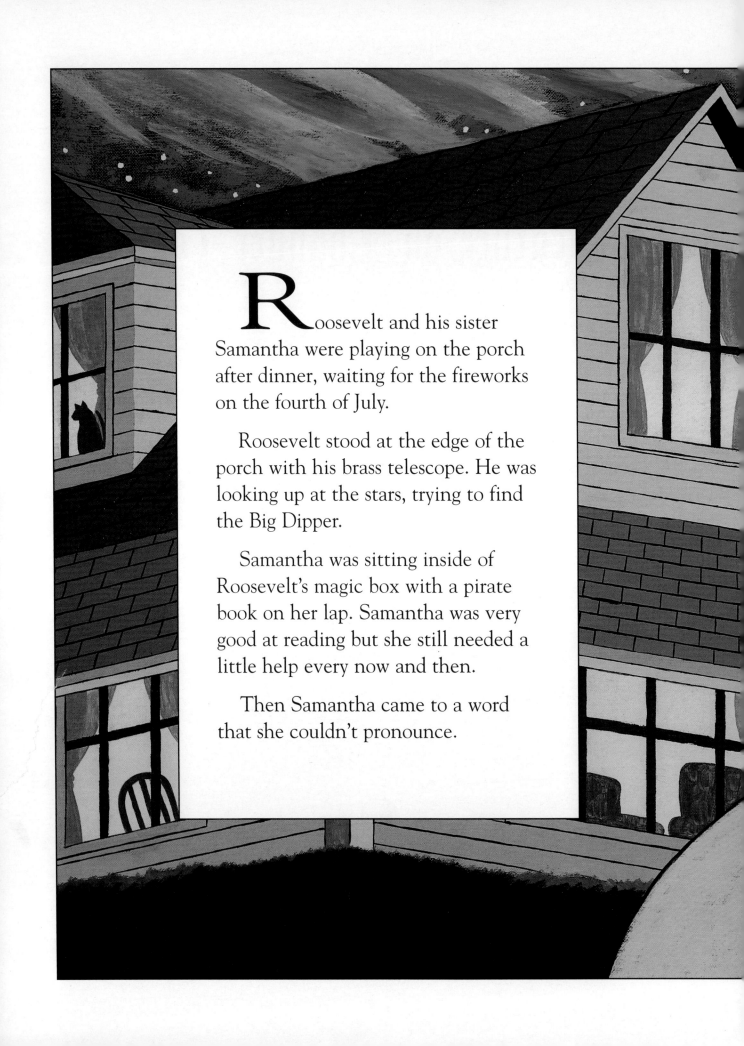

Roosevelt and his sister Samantha were playing on the porch after dinner, waiting for the fireworks on the fourth of July.

Roosevelt stood at the edge of the porch with his brass telescope. He was looking up at the stars, trying to find the Big Dipper.

Samantha was sitting inside of Roosevelt's magic box with a pirate book on her lap. Samantha was very good at reading but she still needed a little help every now and then.

Then Samantha came to a word that she couldn't pronounce.

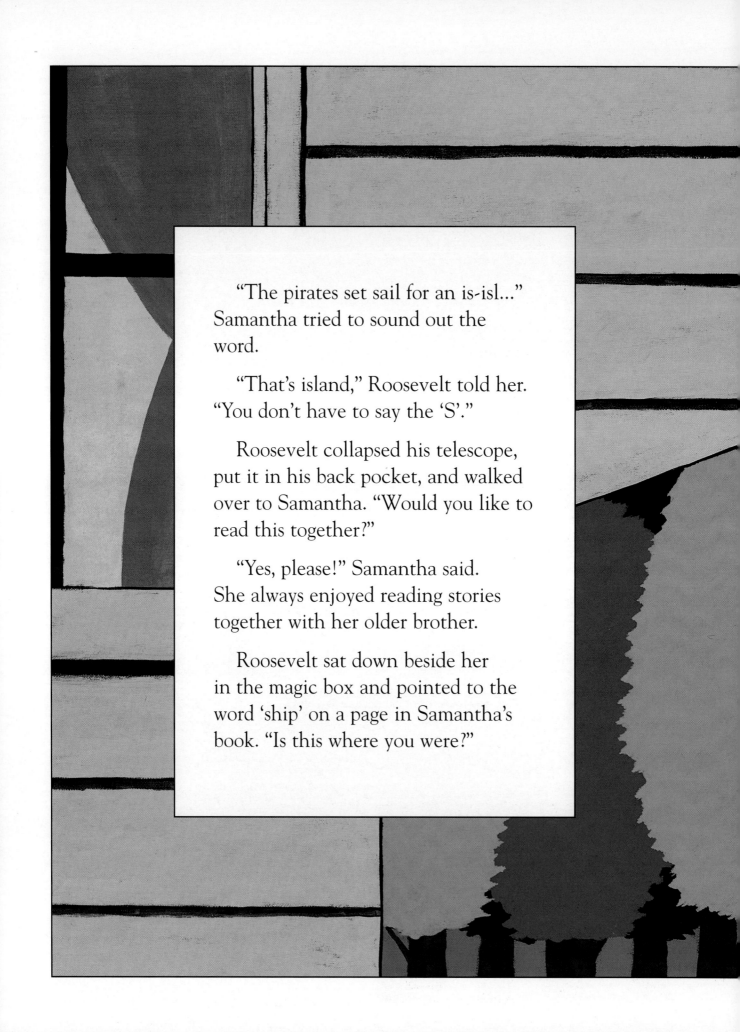

"The pirates set sail for an is-isl..." Samantha tried to sound out the word.

"That's island," Roosevelt told her. "You don't have to say the 'S'."

Roosevelt collapsed his telescope, put it in his back pocket, and walked over to Samantha. "Would you like to read this together?"

"Yes, please!" Samantha said. She always enjoyed reading stories together with her older brother.

Roosevelt sat down beside her in the magic box and pointed to the word 'ship' on a page in Samantha's book. "Is this where you were?"

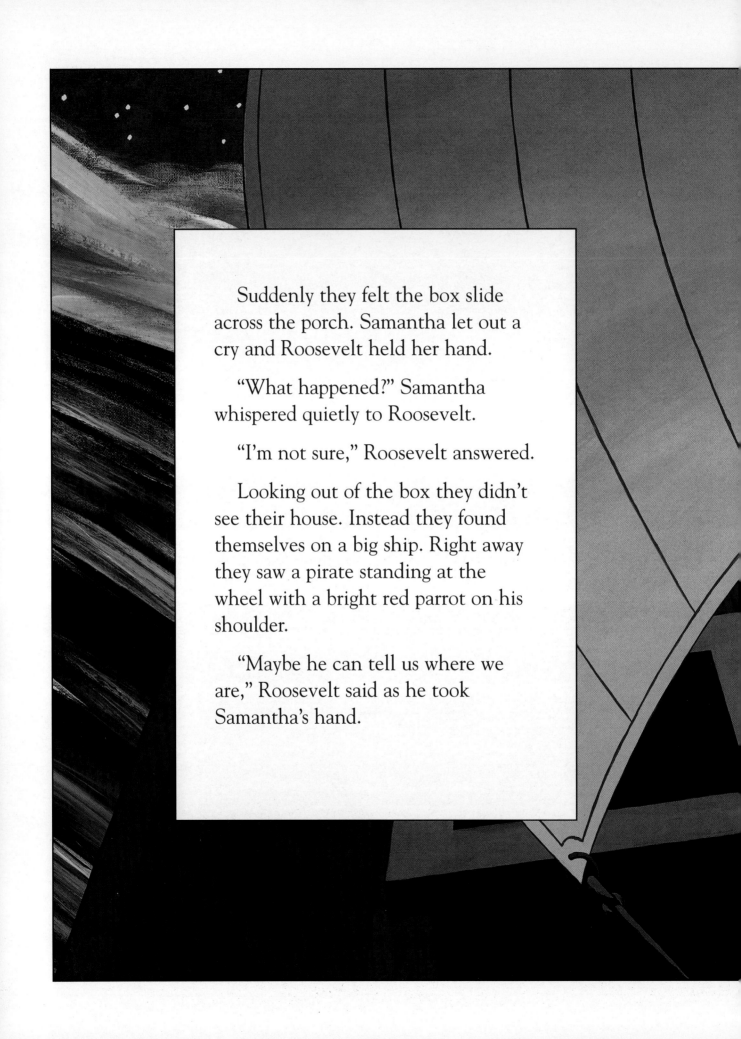

Suddenly they felt the box slide across the porch. Samantha let out a cry and Roosevelt held her hand.

"What happened?" Samantha whispered quietly to Roosevelt.

"I'm not sure," Roosevelt answered.

Looking out of the box they didn't see their house. Instead they found themselves on a big ship. Right away they saw a pirate standing at the wheel with a bright red parrot on his shoulder.

"Maybe he can tell us where we are," Roosevelt said as he took Samantha's hand.

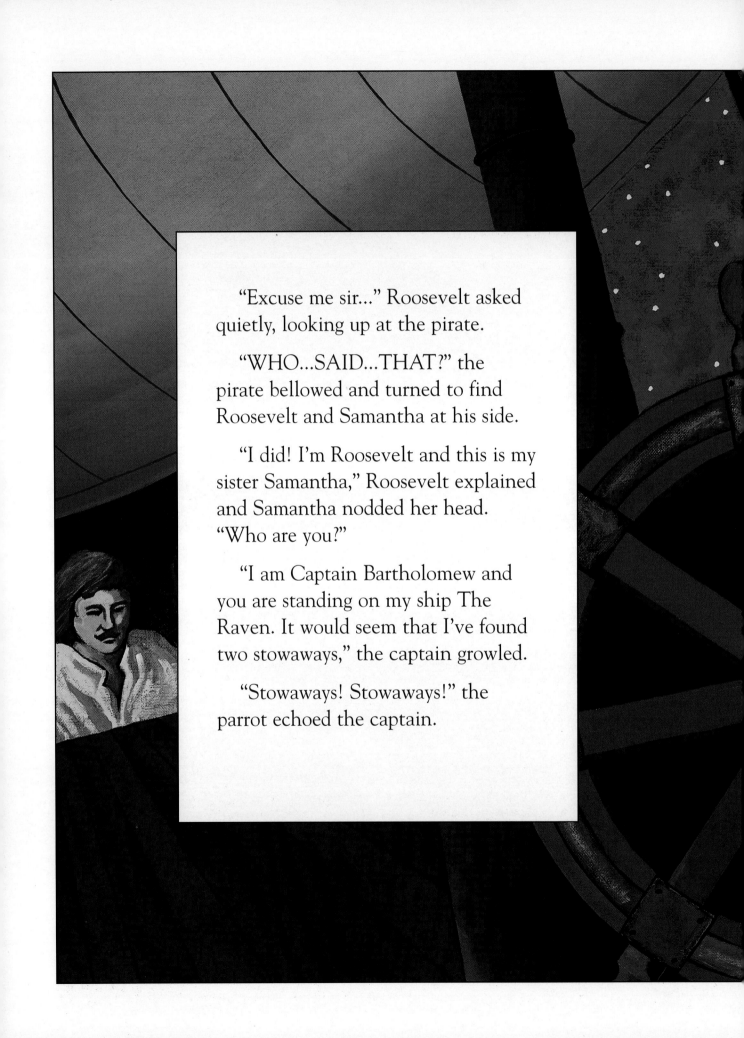

"Excuse me sir..." Roosevelt asked quietly, looking up at the pirate.

"WHO...SAID...THAT?" the pirate bellowed and turned to find Roosevelt and Samantha at his side.

"I did! I'm Roosevelt and this is my sister Samantha," Roosevelt explained and Samantha nodded her head. "Who are you?"

"I am Captain Bartholomew and you are standing on my ship The Raven. It would seem that I've found two stowaways," the captain growled.

"Stowaways! Stowaways!" the parrot echoed the captain.

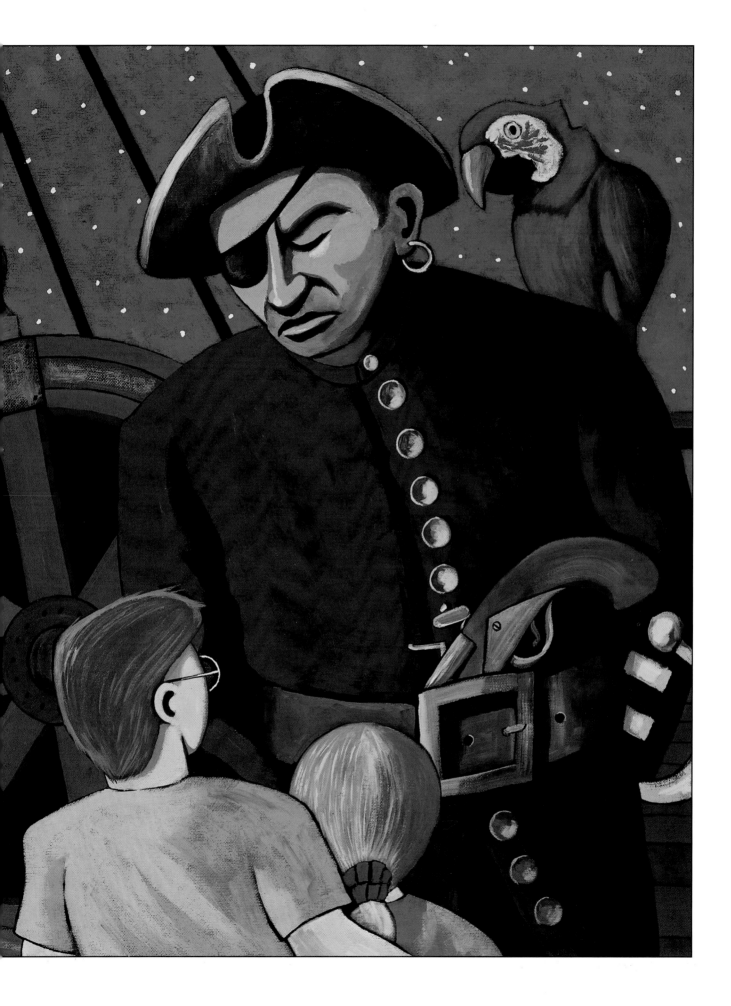

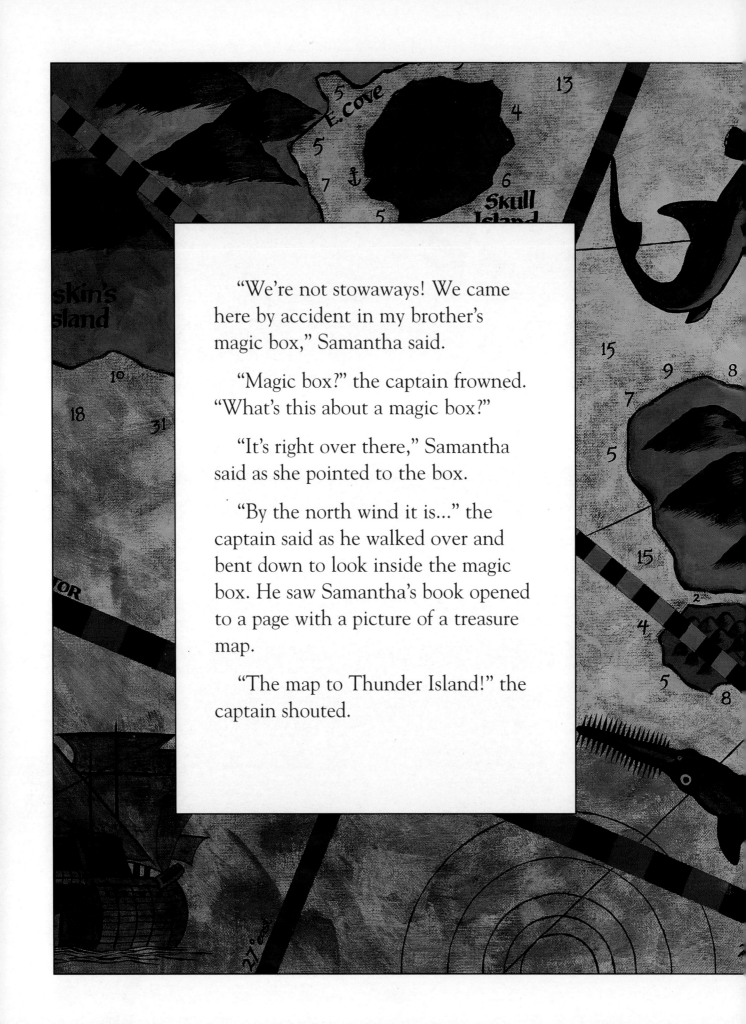

"We're not stowaways! We came here by accident in my brother's magic box," Samantha said.

"Magic box?" the captain frowned. "What's this about a magic box?"

"It's right over there," Samantha said as she pointed to the box.

"By the north wind it is..." the captain said as he walked over and bent down to look inside the magic box. He saw Samantha's book opened to a page with a picture of a treasure map.

"The map to Thunder Island!" the captain shouted.

"Mates! Turn a southern course to Thunder Island! Shiver and shake, there's a fortune to make!" the captain called to his crew.

"Fortune to make! Fortune to make!" the parrot echoed as the crew gave a loud cheer.

The captain turned back to Roosevelt and Samantha. "Usually it's a walk on the plank for stowaways, but you two seem to have earned your keep with this book of yours. So you will be my guests and help me find Thunder Island where the treasure lies. Now both of you come to the galley with me for some supper."

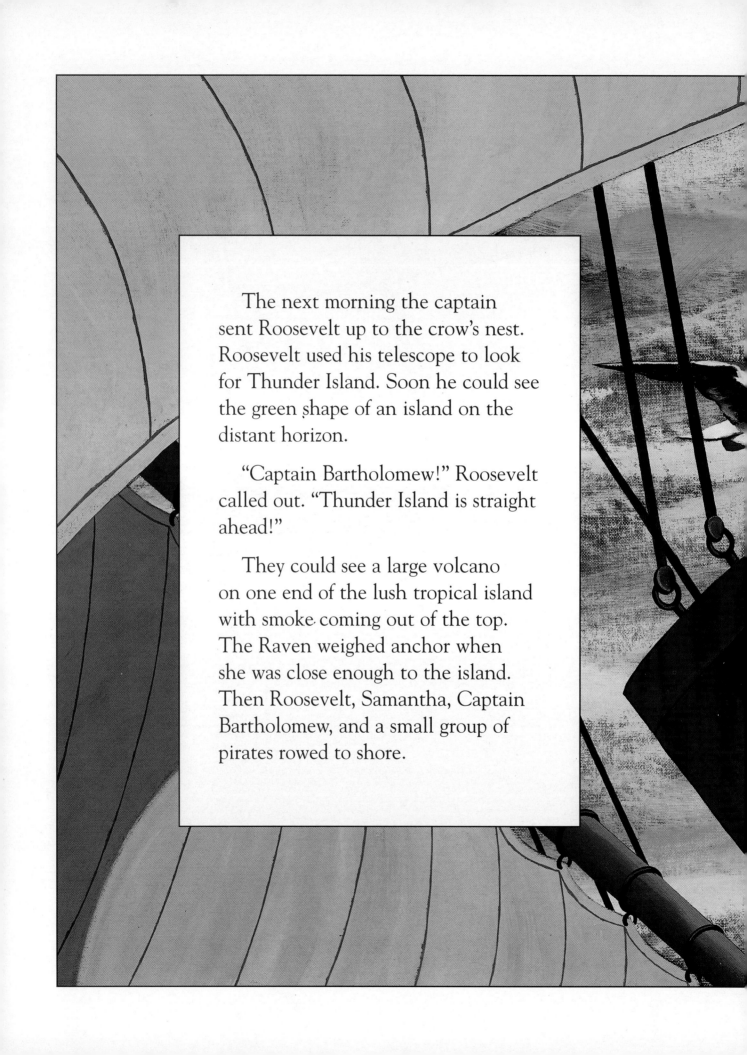

The next morning the captain
sent Roosevelt up to the crow's nest.
Roosevelt used his telescope to look
for Thunder Island. Soon he could see
the green shape of an island on the
distant horizon.

"Captain Bartholomew!" Roosevelt
called out. "Thunder Island is straight
ahead!"

They could see a large volcano
on one end of the lush tropical island
with smoke coming out of the top.
The Raven weighed anchor when
she was close enough to the island.
Then Roosevelt, Samantha, Captain
Bartholomew, and a small group of
pirates rowed to shore.

"We should follow a path that leads north through the trees," Samantha read from her book when they landed on the beach.

Captain Bartholomew pulled out a compass and quickly found the way. The path was marked with an old and tattered pirate flag flying from a tree branch. It looked like no one had walked on the path for many years. They followed the path into the dark woods.

After walking for a little while they came to a fork in the path. They had to choose between two paths, one leading right and one leading left.

"Wait," Samantha said reading from her book. "The map says the right path is da- dan- dangerous!"

But the pirates didn't listen to Samantha and started up the path on the right. They had only taken a few steps when they came to the edge of a cliff hidden by some trees. The pirates in front almost fell over the edge and one man even lost his boot. Looking over the cliff's edge they saw a hidden inlet below with lots of hungry sharks swimming there. One of the sharks gobbled up the lost boot in an instant.

"Samantha was right," the captain said. "Next time we'll listen to her."

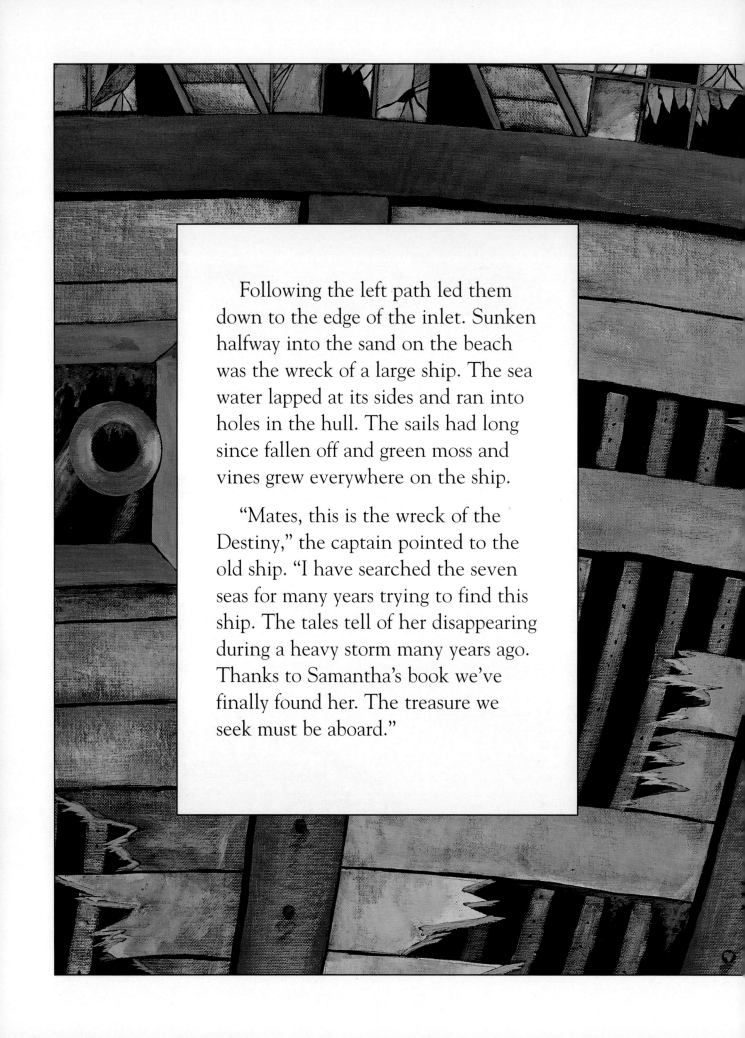

Following the left path led them down to the edge of the inlet. Sunken halfway into the sand on the beach was the wreck of a large ship. The sea water lapped at its sides and ran into holes in the hull. The sails had long since fallen off and green moss and vines grew everywhere on the ship.

"Mates, this is the wreck of the Destiny," the captain pointed to the old ship. "I have searched the seven seas for many years trying to find this ship. The tales tell of her disappearing during a heavy storm many years ago. Thanks to Samantha's book we've finally found her. The treasure we seek must be aboard."

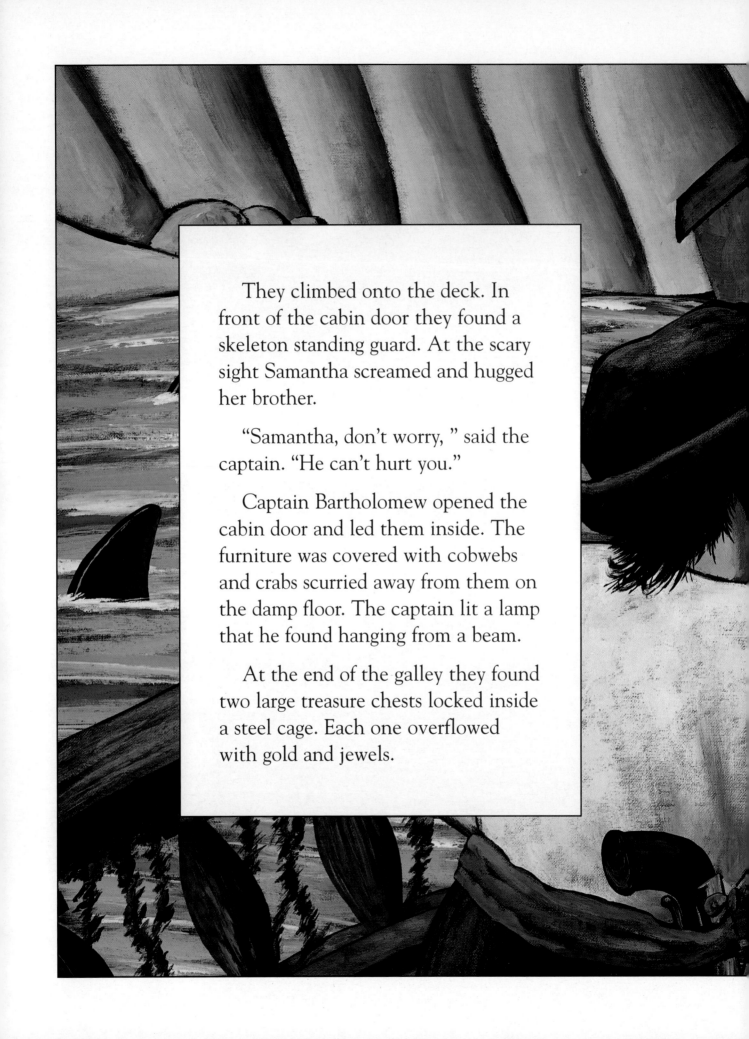

They climbed onto the deck. In front of the cabin door they found a skeleton standing guard. At the scary sight Samantha screamed and hugged her brother.

"Samantha, don't worry, " said the captain. "He can't hurt you."

Captain Bartholomew opened the cabin door and led them inside. The furniture was covered with cobwebs and crabs scurried away from them on the damp floor. The captain lit a lamp that he found hanging from a beam.

At the end of the galley they found two large treasure chests locked inside a steel cage. Each one overflowed with gold and jewels.

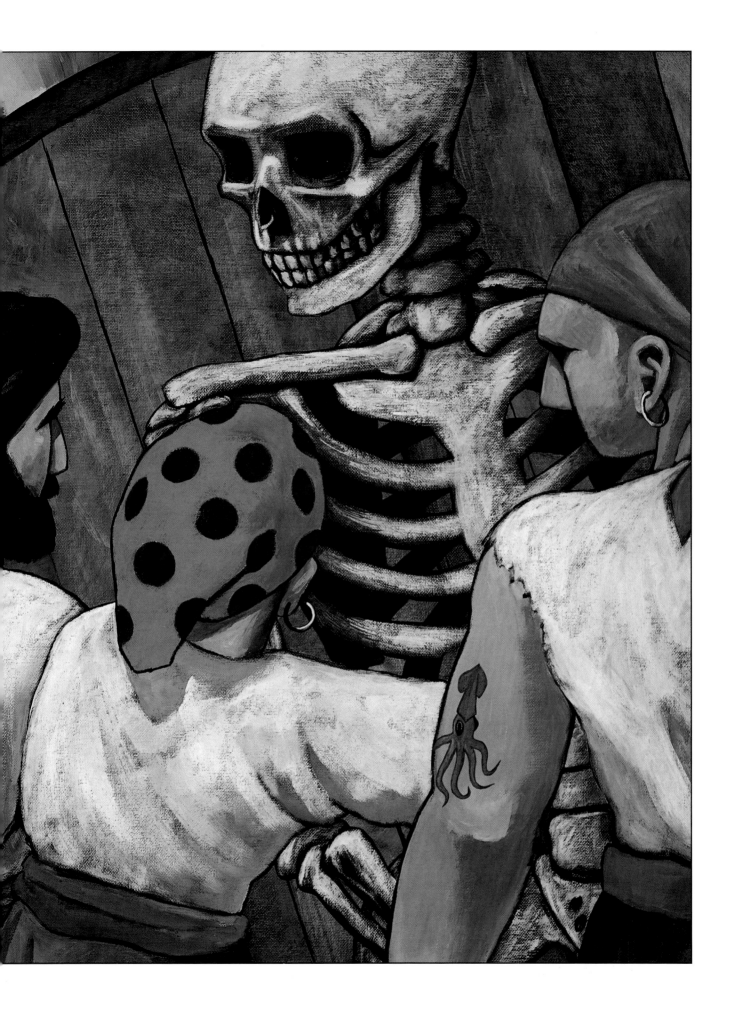

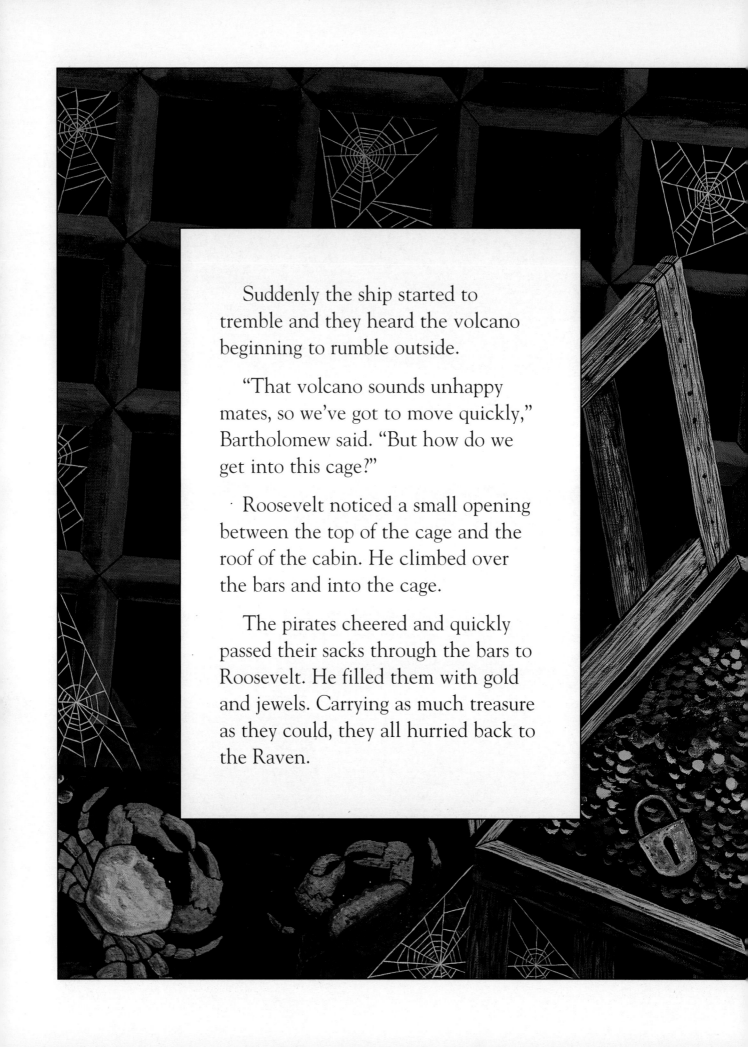

Suddenly the ship started to tremble and they heard the volcano beginning to rumble outside.

"That volcano sounds unhappy mates, so we've got to move quickly," Bartholomew said. "But how do we get into this cage?"

Roosevelt noticed a small opening between the top of the cage and the roof of the cabin. He climbed over the bars and into the cage.

The pirates cheered and quickly passed their sacks through the bars to Roosevelt. He filled them with gold and jewels. Carrying as much treasure as they could, they all hurried back to the Raven.

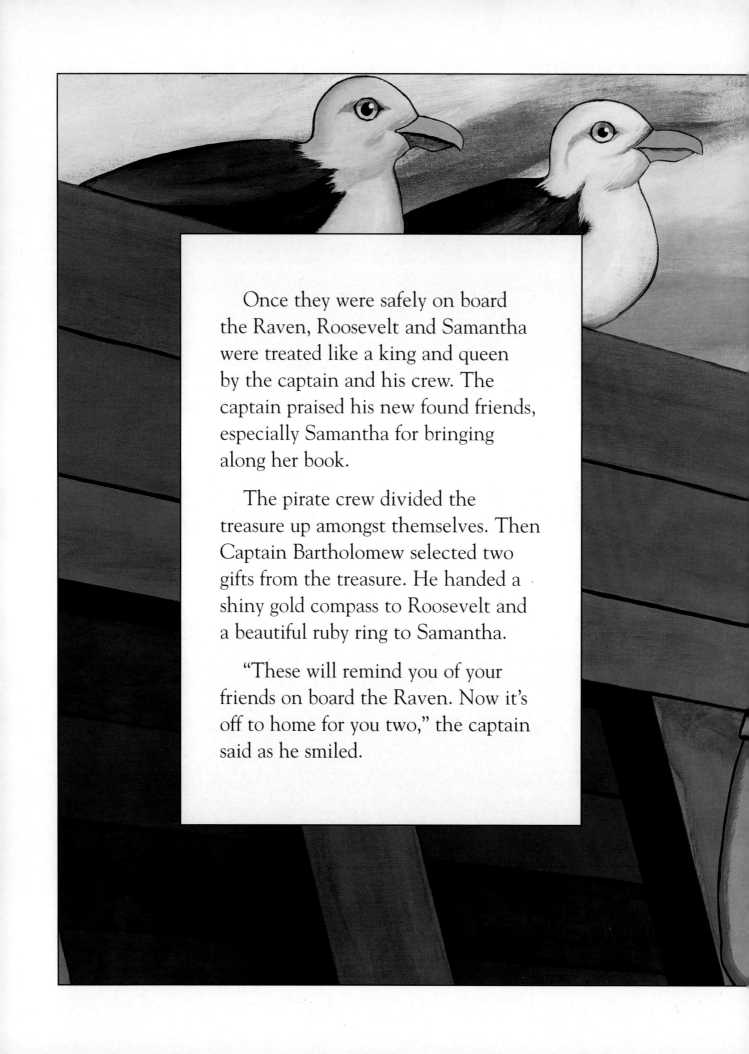

Once they were safely on board the Raven, Roosevelt and Samantha were treated like a king and queen by the captain and his crew. The captain praised his new found friends, especially Samantha for bringing along her book.

The pirate crew divided the treasure up amongst themselves. Then Captain Bartholomew selected two gifts from the treasure. He handed a shiny gold compass to Roosevelt and a beautiful ruby ring to Samantha.

"These will remind you of your friends on board the Raven. Now it's off to home for you two," the captain said as he smiled.

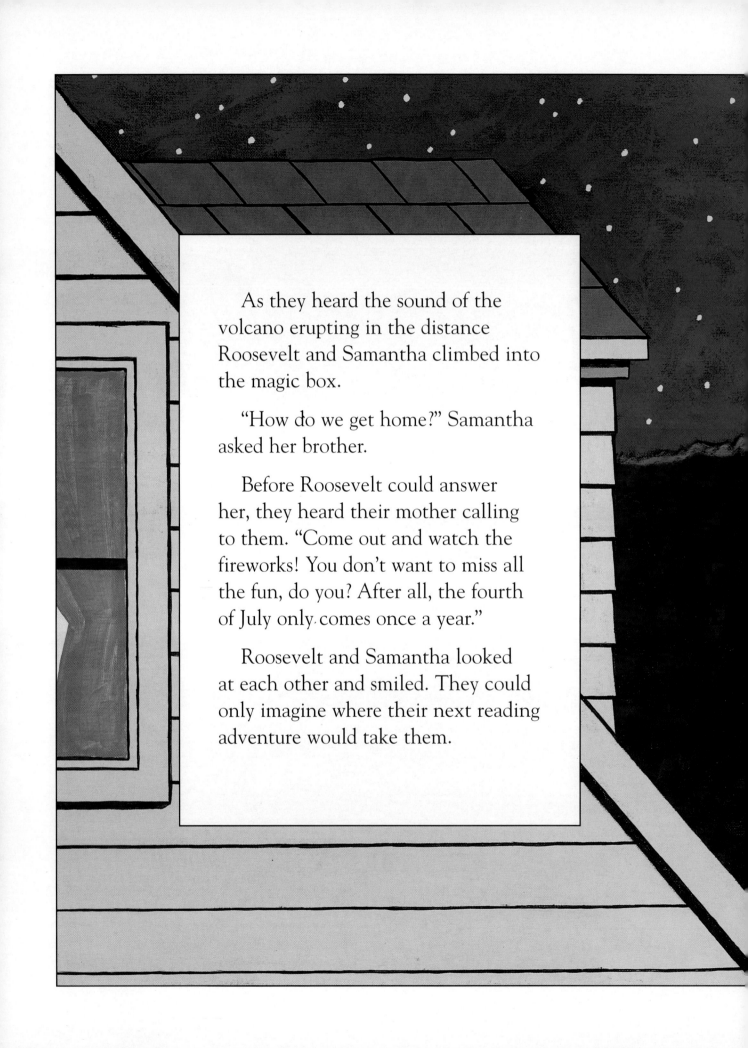

As they heard the sound of the volcano erupting in the distance Roosevelt and Samantha climbed into the magic box.

"How do we get home?" Samantha asked her brother.

Before Roosevelt could answer her, they heard their mother calling to them. "Come out and watch the fireworks! You don't want to miss all the fun, do you? After all, the fourth of July only comes once a year."

Roosevelt and Samantha looked at each other and smiled. They could only imagine where their next reading adventure would take them.

Please send comments and questions to:
Book Buddy Publishing Co., Inc.
16 Lake Oniad Drive
Wappingers Falls, N.Y. 12590

Design and typesetting by Michael Miracle.